In the Ghost Detective Universe:

Novels
(Best to be read in order)
Beyond the Grave
Unveiling the Past
Beneath the Surface

Short Stories
(All stand-alone)
Just Desserts
Lost Friends
Family Bonds
Common Ground
Till Death
Family History
Heritage
Eternal Bond
New Beginnings
Severed Ties

Family Bonds

by R.W. Wallace

Copyright © 2021 by R.W. Wallace

Copy editing by Jinxie Gervasio
Cover by R.W. Wallace
Cover Illustration 10926765 © germanjames | 123rf.com
Cover Illustration 1431114 © Alain Frechette | pexels
Cover Illustration 263199440 © Nouman | Adobe Stock

All characters and events in this book, other than those clearly in the public domain, are fictitious and any resemblance to real persons, living or dead, is purely coincidental.

All rights reserved. No part of this publication may be reproduced, distributed, or transmitted in any form or by any means, including photocopying, recording, or other electronic or mechanical methods, without the prior written permission of the publisher, except in the case of brief quotations embodied in critical reviews and certain other noncommercial uses permitted by copyright law.

www.rwwallace.com

ISBN: [979-10-95707-17-2]

Main category—Fiction
Other category—Mystery

First Edition

R.W. WALLACE

Author of the Tolosa Mystery Series

FAMILY BONDS

A Ghost Detective Short Story

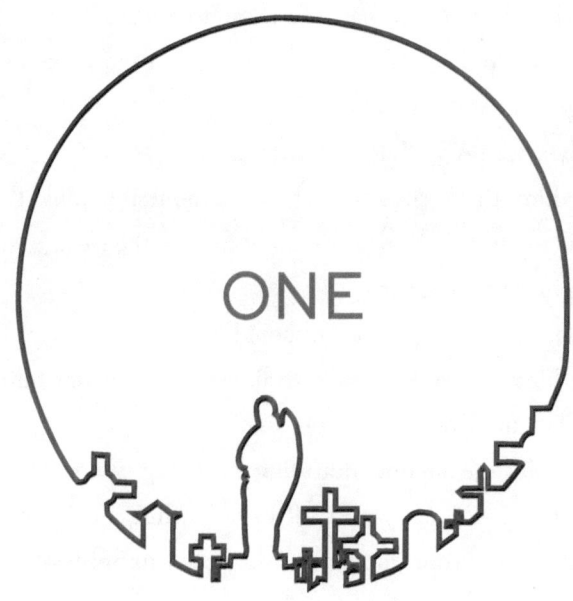

ONE

I'VE BEEN FEELING terribly lonely lately. Not surprising really, when you live in a cemetery.

I'm usually not the only ghost to haunt this particular ground. Some people come and go as they rise from their urns or caskets, deal with their unfinished business, and leave for what I assume to be a better place.

Two of us have become something of a fixture. Personally, I've been here for over thirty years, and have yet to obtain that elusive closure one needs to move on. Clothilde, my moody twenty-year-old companion, has haunted this spot since the mid-eighties. She was here before me.

We usually attend funerals together, greet the new arrivals together. It's good to be part of a team, to have someone complementary to do the jobs I can't do. She might behave like a moody teenager, but she's a good person.

She's been AWOL for three days.

I don't think she's moved on—I honestly think I'd have known about it, both the process of finding the closure, and the fading into nothing part.

No, she's hiding—and I'm bored.

I think we have a new arrival. An old lady was buried on Thursday, and I've been hearing sounds.

Usually, the old ones don't linger for long. When you see the end coming, you get your stuff in order, line up the ducks for your heirs, say your goodbyes. Not much unfinished business, except with the really bone-headed ones.

The normal thing to do when you discover you're stuck in a casket six feet below the ground, is to scream. Pound. Call for help.

This lady—Bernadette Humbert according to the name penciled in on the temporary wooden cross on her grave—isn't screaming.

But she's *there*.

I can hear her scratching at the casket, talking to herself, even singing.

If she's not let out of the casket, it means she has not yet accepted that she's become a ghost. She's awfully cozy for someone who thinks she's buried alive.

A hand bursts through the dirt, quickly followed by a head.

Old lady, indeed. She has one of those hair-dos that seem molded in place no matter what you do to it. Slight curl, lots of volume, ideal lodging place for a beehive. Lots of wrinkles and excess skin, but if I heard correctly during the funeral, she was eighty-two, so it's all par for the course. I'd say she has more worry lines than laugh lines, though.

"Oh!" she says as she bursts free. "There we are. Hello, young man. How do you do?"

"Hello, Ma'am," I reply and tip an imaginary hat. "Robert Villemur, at your service."

She nods regally and pulls herself up far enough to free her torso. She looks around, taking in the cemetery, currently bathed in brilliant winter sunshine. "I assume you are also a ghost, Robert. Are there others like us here?"

She's not even out of the grave yet, and she's already assessing her environment, looking for potential dangers. I think I like her.

"Only two resident ghosts at the moment," I say. "Three, now, including you. But my friend has apparently decided to take some alone time." I shrug. "She'll be back eventually."

Bernadette nods in satisfaction and crawls the rest of the way out of the grave. She seems to have already grasped the concept of being a ghost, where your mind decides what's physical and what isn't. To get out of the grave, you need to imagine footholds to step out, but the dirt you're moving through can't hold you back.

Even crawling, there's a certain dignity to the way this woman holds herself up. I'm guessing she's one of those people for whom appearances are everything.

She stands up, flicking non-existing dirt from her

green-and-white checkered pantsuit. "I must admit, I'd expect more than two ghosts in such a large cemetery. Are there not regular new arrivals?"

I keep my eyes on her, hands in my pockets, to gauge her reaction. "Oh, there are funerals aplenty. But only the people with unfinished business linger."

One eyebrow arches up, but I also catch the twitch below her right eye. "You insinuate I have unfinished business?"

I give a nonchalant shrug. "If you don't figure out what it is, I'm afraid you'll be here for a really long time, Ma'am. The only situation in which I've seen anyone move on, is when they wrapped up some loose end they'd left dangling before dying."

She draws herself up, gaining a good inch or two—nice, she already masters the standing-on-air thing—and looks down her nose at me. "Well, I never. You have some nerve making accusations of the kind. And we only just met!"

"I'm not making accusations, Bernadette," I tell her, and have to admit to a certain thrill on seeing the shock on her face when I use her first name. "I am stating fact. Now, I'll just go hang out in my little corner of the cemetery." I point to the cheapest section, where both mine and Clothilde's graves lie. "If you want to talk, I'm here. It would be my pleasure to assist you in finding closure."

I turn and walk away while she's still gathering steam, humming a toneless tune to myself as I go.

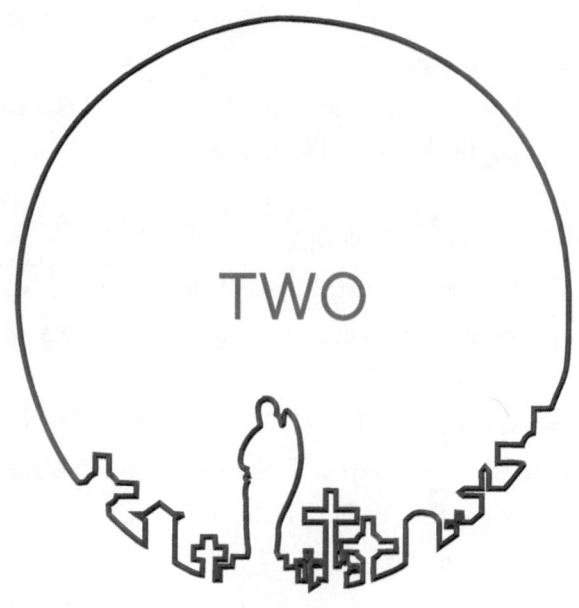

TWO

It takes her two days to come around. I'm on the verge of going looking for her myself because I'm so bored. Clothilde hasn't shown her face for five days, and I'm actually getting worried. Helping out Bernadette would at least keep my mind occupied.

Bernadette takes almost an hour to amble across the cemetery grounds to reach me. She takes her sweet time, stopping to look at the different graves, tombstones, and mausoleums, attempting—but failing—to flick away dirt on the less maintained ones.

Finally, she comes to a stop in front of me, where I'm leaning against Clothilde's tombstone, as usual.

"I can't leave the cemetery," she states. She stands with her hands folded in front of her, an old lady's purse swinging from one arm. Nice touch.

"No," I say. "We can't leave the cemetery. Nobody has ever managed that. Believe me, we've all tried."

"There aren't any other ghosts."

"I'm afraid you're stuck with me, Ma'am."

"I don't understand why I'm still here." Her stance stays the same, and there's no hint of emotion in her eyes. "I do not have any unfinished business."

I consider the possibility of just letting her believe that and send her on her way. So what if she's too stubborn to admit she might have regrets? It shouldn't be my problem.

Except it kind of is.

If she doesn't address her issues, she's going to stay here. And I might be bored right now, but I don't think someone like Bernadette is going to make my life in the cemetery any better. Quite the contrary.

Also, I have to help her. It's my self-designated duty to help the other ghosts move on.

It's my only hope for redemption.

"I'm not here to pry into your personal business, Bernadette," I say, my voice soft. "But I'm willing to help if you want it."

She sniffs but doesn't leave. After a pause, "What kind of unfinished business are we talking about? I simply do not see what it could be."

"The most common one is simply not having said goodbye to a loved one," I tell her. "As long as the person comes to visit the grave at some point, the ghost usually moves on very quickly."

She shakes her head.

"In second place, we have unsolved murders. Most people—naturally enough—can't rest in peace"—pun totally intended—"until their murderer is caught and brought to justice. That one's honestly tricky to manage when we're stuck in the cemetery and can't interact with people, but mostly, we manage. And quite often, the police actually do their jobs, and once the ghosts learn the murderer is caught, they move on."

Bernadette sniffs and lifts her nose a little higher. "I died of a heart-attack in my bed, young man."

"Right." I smile as if her attitude doesn't bother me—and it doesn't. People like Bernadette didn't bother or intimidate me when I was alive; they certainly won't when we're both ghosts. "You asked me about unfinished business. I'm simply giving you our most common cases, to see if we find a match."

I start to pace back and forth, mostly to force Bernadette to swing from side to side to follow me with her eyes. "I'd say children come in third. It can be leaving them a mess of an inheritance, not leaving them anything and regretting it, not telling them they were good enough. The list goes on. Did you have children, Bernadette?"

"I have a son. Guillaume. But there are no regrets."

I stop pacing and stand right in front of Bernadette. It's difficult to look down your nose as someone towering a head above you.

"You hesitated," I say. "Before saying you have a son."

Bernadette says nothing. Pinches her lips together.

"What?" I don't let her break our eye contact. "Did something happen to your son? No? Was there just the one?"

Her right eye twitches.

"Come now, Bernadette. You can tell me. Who will I tell?" I indicate the empty cemetery around us. "Did you have a child you had to give away when you were young? A child who lived with his father and you never tried to get in touch?"

"Don't be ridiculous," she scolds me. "Do you realize what you are accusing me of? I will *not* stand for this type of treatment!"

I'm tempted to ask her if she's planning on going to the police but restrain myself. I keep my voice low. "Then why don't you tell me what really happened. You had a second child?"

She resists, but not for long. If I read her correctly, she's realizing this might be the reason she's still stuck here and getting out might be worth the bother of telling me her story.

"I had a daughter," she finally says. "She died a long time ago, leaving behind an unprecedented mess that I had to clean up." There's fire in her eyes now. "*Her* wanting to apologize to *me* for what she did I'd understand. But *not* the other way around."

I can't help it, I'm hooked. "What did she do?"

Bernadette's voice has achieved that calm that means it's best to get far, far away. "She took out two careers, one family, and an entire city council with one cut."

Okay. I need to hear this story. But first things first. "What was her name?"

She spits the word out. "Clothilde."

Oh.

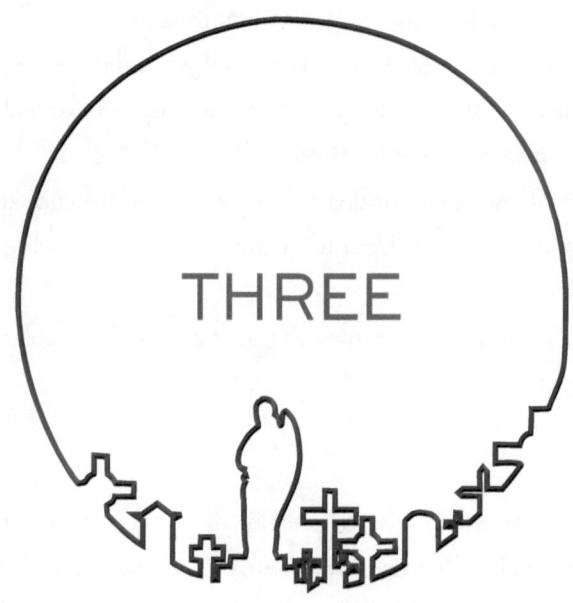

THREE

I STAND THERE, my mouth hanging open, as thoughts jumble around in my head.

Clothilde.

This is Clothilde's mother. She *has* to be.

This is why Clothilde hasn't shown her face since the funeral. She knew it was her mother and doesn't want to meet her.

Now, the question is: can we get two birds with one stone? Can they find closure together?

My chest pinches at the thought of losing my friend of thirty years, but I can't wish for her to stay here any longer than necessary. If her mother being here is what she needs to move on, I'll make it happen.

I'll need a little more information, though.

I paste on a polite smile. "Perhaps if you tell me exactly what happened, I can give an opinion? Sometimes, an external viewpoint can see what the involved parties cannot."

She doesn't look thrilled at the idea, but in the end, keeping up appearances after death is less important than moving on to the afterlife.

"Clothilde took her own life in the most spectacular way," she says.

༄

She was found in a hotel room in the city center, not too far from City Hall. The room was poorly lit and moldy, the hotel so structurally unsound it'd been demolished a mere year later, and the staff particularly unhelpful—by talking too much in some cases, by not saying a word in others.

Both her wrists had been slit, the razor blade she'd used on the floor next to the bed. She lay spread out on the bed like Jesus on the Cross, her feet at the headboard, her arms hanging out so the blood fell directly to the floor, and her head lolling over the foot of the bed so that the first thing people would see when they came through the door, was her dead eyes.

The man who'd rented the room hadn't used his real name, of course, but it hadn't taken much digging to discover it was one of the city's most prominent lawyers. The desk clerk described him perfectly, telling the police he'd arrived with Clothilde just before lunch, then left alone about an hour later.

Having a less-than-stellar desk clerk's word against the lawyer's wouldn't be proof enough, of course. His card with a scribbled date and hour—the day of the death, eleven thirty—on the back in the lawyer's handwriting, stuffed into Clothilde's back pocket, didn't help.

His hair and fingerprints all over the room, even less so.

Clothilde didn't have just the one card with her. She also had the number of the City Council's Vice President.

This was where the desk clerk came off as a somewhat credible witness and denied ever seeing the Vice President in his hotel. He *had* seen another man come and go, one who hadn't checked into the hotel but claimed to be there just for a visit, but it was someone else.

Someone they never identified.

Needless to say, once the media got hold of the story, it all blew up.

A link was found between the lawyer and the Vice President—the lawyer had helped the other man buy the silence of two previous mistresses.

One of the mistresses was the daughter of another City Council member, currently married to a prominent financial mogul.

An internal war broke out within the City Council, some blaming their colleague for seducing a younger, married woman, some blaming the woman's father for not bringing her up right. The fight brought to light a slew of wrongdoings for all parties, and the entire City Council ended up being forced to retire.

The financial mogul divorced his wife, leaving her with nothing, not even their two children. He kept the parental rights, but completely neglected the poor kids, who went from nanny to nanny until he shipped them off to boarding school in England.

Clothilde's father, who had worked as an assistant for the Mayor, lost his job once it became clear how large the political impact would become. On a fast track to higher responsibilities, his career had taken a nose-dive. He'd never managed to get more than a position as a dentist's secretary, and most of their friends had cut all contact.

"What about Clothilde?" I ask once Bernadette finishes her story.

"What about Clothilde? She was dead. Selfishly killed herself and did as much damage as possible on the way out."

"But..." I furrow my brow in confusion. "I agree it *could* have been suicide. But it could also have been murder."

Bernadette sniffs. "It wasn't. A police officer was brought in to look into it, and concluded—quite quickly, I might add—that it was suicide."

Something scratches at a memory while Bernadette tells her story. Something about the hotel. "Do you remember the name of the establishment in which Clothilde was found?"

"Of course I do," Bernadette replies frostily. "It's the one just across from the train station. *Hôtel de la gare.*"

Memories come swarming back. My superior officer telling me he needs me to go check out a suicide in a hotel. Everybody knows it was a suicide, but someone needs to make an official inquiry and conclusion. He feels confident I'm the man for the job.

Happy with another easy case, I go to the hotel, make a quick check under the bed and in the bathroom, peek at the now-empty bed where the victim had lain spread out, make sure the lock wasn't forced, and conclude it was a suicide.

I never even bothered going to the morgue to see the body.

"What importance is the name of the hotel?" Bernadette asks, bringing me back to the present.

"It's not," I reply, my throat dry. "Just curious."

"As you can see," she says, clearly not catching on to my internal struggle, "there is no reason for me to have unfinished business with my daughter. We gave her everything growing up—love, education, a roof over her head—and she repays us by taking her own life and ruining our lives and that of many others in the process."

I force my self-flagellating thoughts to the back of my mind to look at later, and concentrate on the woman before me, and the reason she is still here.

"Did you immediately believe your daughter took her own life?" I ask.

Bernadette purses her lips. "What does it matter what I thought. She did it. Ruined everything."

I shift against the tombstone behind me, where I've been standing since I discovered who Bernadette is, wanting to move around to walk off the feeling of ants covering my body, but not wanting to display to Bernadette the name on the stone—Clothilde.

I take a deep breath. Let it out slowly. The exercise doesn't help much when you don't have a real body.

"What if she didn't?" I ask. "What if she was murdered?"

Bernadette sniffs. "Don't be ridiculous. The police investigated and concluded it was suicide."

"What if they were wrong?" I couldn't bring myself to tell her I'd been the officer to "investigate." This was why I'd been stuck here for so long—I had a lot of sloppy police work to make up for.

"That's not…" She shifts from one foot to the other. "They wouldn't…" Her handbag disappears, only to reappear a second later. "How would I even… They told me she did it herself!"

"Did you believe them?" I ask her, my voice calm. "What did your heart tell you?"

She stares at me for a long time, a deepening worry line cutting across her forehead, her eyes distant.

When she finally answers, her voice is a mere whisper. "What mother would believe her daughter wished to kill herself? It's impossible to contemplate." She swallows. "She was such a difficult child, so headstrong. So rebellious."

I nod. That does sound like the Clothilde I know.

"She told me she was going to do something big," Bernadette says. "Something that would make an impact in our city." Her gaze focuses on me. "Her killing herself most definitely had an impact on our city. The entire City Council had to step down."

Grief seems to swamp her for a moment, then she shakes it off and squares her shoulders. "In the end, I concluded this was what her plan had been all along. Though I never understood why." Her voice cracks on the last word.

I wonder where Clothilde is currently hiding. Is she at the other end of the cemetery, as far away from us as possible? Or is she hanging around here, listening in on our conversation?

Sadly enough, even after spending thirty years together, I don't know her well enough to tell.

I do know she has unfinished business, or she wouldn't still be here. I'm starting to get an inkling of what it might be.

"How would it make you feel if you learned your daughter didn't kill herself?" I ask.

The handbag disappears, and Bernadette puts her hand to her heart. "If she didn't kill herself, it means someone else murdered her."

I nod.

"But… That's…" Her entire shape flickers, the stress coursing through her making her forget her form at times.

I keep my voice low and soft. "How would that make you feel?"

A tear trickles down Bernadette's cheek. "My poor baby. It means I failed her!" She takes two steps toward me, her fake dignity long forgotten. "She didn't even get a proper funeral."

I open my arms and let her come into my embrace. "I think I might know what you need to move on, Bernadette," I say into her hair. "But there's something I need to check on first. Will you be all right while I do my investigation?"

She calms down fairly quickly, considering. Stepping away from me, she pulls on the lapels of her jacket. "I'll be fine, young man." She studies her handbag, which is back in place. "I wonder if I could get hold of my knitting…"

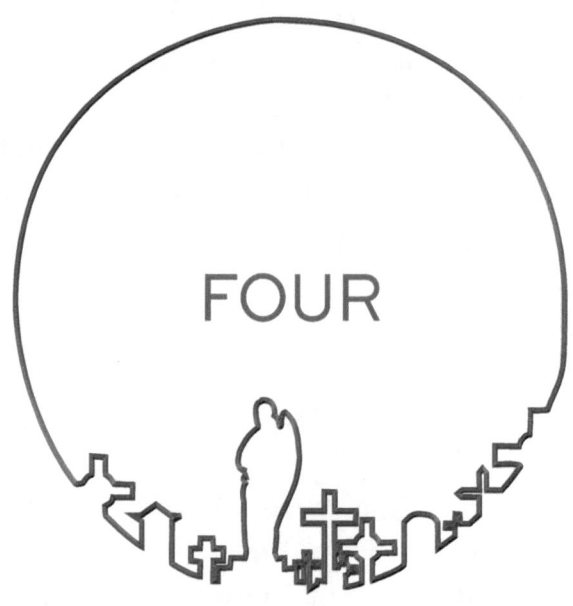

FOUR

Once Bernadette is out of earshot, I shove away from Clothilde's tombstone and sit down on top of my own grave.

"Clothilde?" I say softly. "I know you're nearby. Will you please come out?"

For a long time, nothing happens. Although I'm burning up with alternating guilt and curiosity, I stay put, giving her the time she needs to show herself.

Finally, well into the next day, she comes. One moment I can't see her; the next, she sits on the tombstone, her Converse-clad feet dangling.

She doesn't talk to me. Doesn't look at me.

"I met your mother," I say. "Lovely woman."

The snort escapes before she can catch it.

My lips curl into a soft smile. "I understand why you've been avoiding her, Clothilde. But I think she needs your help."

Another snort. "Right."

"If she's here," I say, "it means she has unfinished business. I'm pretty sure it involves you. And the circumstances around your death."

Clothilde lifts her eyes to meet mine for the first time since her mother's funeral. They are duller than usual, less focused. Sad.

"She abandoned me," she says, her voice low but steady. "Somebody suggested I'd taken my own life, and she believed them. Couldn't even offer me a place with the rest of the family." She kicks at the tombstone with one heel.

I nod. "I know that's how it looks," I tell my friend. "But you've been here even longer than me, Clothilde. How do we know what people's unfinished business is?"

Her lips curl. "We don't. They tell us."

Nodding, I give her a smile. "They know what it is. Sometimes it's obvious to them and us. Sometimes we have to help them figure it out. But they never discover they have unfinished business because we tell them they do."

"That is what she claims."

"It is." I fold my hands in my lap. "I think she's still suffering from the same denial as when she lived. But deep down? She knows she failed you."

Clothilde stares at me with her dull eyes. She's stopped swinging her legs and sits stock still, as if she's a newly added statue to her own tombstone.

"Bullshit," she says.

"She wouldn't be here if she didn't have regrets," I argue. "I think what she needs, is to admit she was wrong to believe what was said about you—and probably have a chat with you."

"Bullshit." A whisper now.

My eyes wander to her tombstone. The simple slab of rock with only her first name on it.

"Who paid for your funeral?" I ask. "You don't exactly have the most coveted spot, but you're here. Despite being listed as a suicide. Who pulled that off?"

Clothilde's eyes search out to the church spire. "I don't know. I only came out of the casket after they'd filled in the hole, and nobody ever came to visit."

My eyebrows shoot up. "You came out straight away?" Most people—me included—spend days screaming before coming to terms with being a ghost.

Clothilde shrugs. "Guess you could say I saw the murder coming. Wasn't surprised to end up dead. Kind of surprised to end up a ghost." A faint smiled flickers across her lips.

I return her smile. "So, we don't know who killed you, we don't know who paid for your funeral, and we don't know what you need to move on?"

Clothilde meets my eyes, her look that of someone who's seen too much. "Two out of three, Detective."

"You know what you need to get out of here?" We've known each other for almost thirty years, and she never shared this fact with me?

She rolls her eyes, reverting back to the rebellious teenager. "I kind of know who killed me," she said. "It's one of two guys—or possibly both of them together." She shrugs. "Doesn't really matter."

I refrain from calling her a liar. Won't do us any good.

"Maybe your mother can help with figuring out who killed you," I say.

"Yeah, right." Clothilde snorts. Her gaze turns in the direction of her mother's grave. Her eyes widen.

Clothilde disappears.

Sighing, I turn to see Bernadette coming down the hill from her grave, walking straight toward me this time.

"Who is your friend?" she asks when she comes closer. "I do hope I didn't scare her away."

I stay silent and let my gaze travel to Clothilde's tombstone, clearly visible to Bernadette now that I'm not hiding the writing.

A sharp intake of breath. "Clo—?" Bernadette whips around, searching the cemetery for her daughter. "She's here? This is where he buried her?"

"Who buried her?" I ask.

Hand on her heart, Bernadette continues scanning our surroundings. "My brother. I gave him some money and asked for him to take care of it." She falls to her knees in front of the tombstone. "It doesn't even say her last name, or her date of birth."

"Is there any chance he didn't want anyone to find her?" I ask. An uncle should know the girl's name and birthday.

Bernadette shakes her head, but more in incomprehension than as an answer to my question.

Her eyes snap up to meet mine. "She's here? As a ghost?"

I don't like ratting out on my friend, but Bernadette has a right to know—and Clothilde can't hide forever. I nod.

"She's been here all this time?" She surges to her feet, clearly caring as little about physical laws as her daughter. "You said only the ones with unfinished business linger."

I nod. I seem to be doing that a lot lately.

"She's been dead for almost thirty years! What's the business she still hasn't finished?"

"I wouldn't know, Ma'am," I say calmly. "She has never deigned to tell me."

Some of the air goes out of Bernadette, her eyes returning to her daughter's name on the tombstone. "That does sound like Clothilde." Her voice breaks. "My poor baby."

I wait for Bernadette to decide on a course of action.

She spends a long time staring at her daughter's grave. Finally, she says, "Clothilde? Can you hear me?"

Silence.

"I'm so terribly sorry, baby. I should never have doubted you." Bernadette swallows as a tear streaks down her face. "You were such a difficult youth and I was too tired. When they told me you probably did it out of spite, I just… I guess it was easier to believe them." Her hands lift, then fall back in defeat. "I guess it took less energy to believe them than to believe in you, my darling. And I'm so, so sorry."

"It's not my fault you were always tired," Clothilde suddenly says. She appears behind her tombstone, using the cold stone as a barrier between herself and her mother.

The longing in Bernadette's eyes made my own eyes fill with tears. "No, darling, it wasn't your fault." A faint smile. "Not too much, anyway."

"You were always too tired," Clothilde continues. "Too tired to help me with my school work. Too tired to organize a proper birthday when I turned eighteen. Too tired to notice I wasn't doing so great."

"I'm sorry I didn't notice, Clo."

"Did you at least manage to sleep better once you didn't have me to worry about?"

Bernadette's hand goes to her handbag and she shakes her head. "I haven't been able to sleep through the night without medication since you died."

I half-expect Clothilde to be happy about this, but she frowns and bites her lip.

Bernadette's eyes go distant, as if she's looking inward. "Now that I think about it, I realize I must have been in some kind of haze for thirty years. I never really made it out after we lost you." She looks to me. "It's gone now. My brain is working properly for the first time in so long."

I nod. "Your brain is no longer hampered by whatever your body's influence was. Nor by medication. Makes sense."

Bernadette's breath catches. "This is my unfinished business," she tells her daughter. "I know I wronged you, darling. And I apologize."

Again, she turns to me. "Is there nothing else I can do for her?"

I shrug. "We have a rather limited field of action, I'm afraid.

Is your business only with Clothilde, or also with the person who killed her?"

Her head snaps to look to her daughter. "Who killed you?"

"I don't know," Clothilde answers, her voice unusually calm. "I have theories."

"Of course, you do," Bernadette says with a genuine smile. "You were always full of those."

And one of the theories probably got her killed.

I keep my mouth shut. Not the time.

Bernadette carefully takes two steps toward her daughter. "I'm sure you'll figure it out, sweetheart. You always were a smart girl. Much smarter than your silly mother."

Clothilde stays behind the tombstone, but her eyes take on a longing it hurts to watch. "You were never silly, Mom."

Bernadette huffs. "Sounds better than stupid."

A snort from Clothilde.

Tentatively, Bernadette holds her arms out toward her daughter. "Will you give your poor, stupid, silly mother a hug? I've missed you terribly."

It's a good thing we can't feel the cold, or hunger, because Clothilde takes her sweet time about answering her mother.

Bernadette stays put, her arms out, waiting.

Finally, Clothilde caves, and flies into her mother's arms.

I want to give them their privacy, but Clothilde says, "Stay," so I do.

When they separate, Bernadette starts fading, as if she's an old drawing left out in the sun for too long.

"I believe you've found your closure," I tell her. "Any last words for your daughter before you move on?"

Surprise on her face, Bernadette stares down at herself, where she will be able to see the ground through her legs and feet. "This is it?" She grabs hold of Clothilde's arm. "What about you? Why aren't you fading, too?"

Clothilde pats her mother's hand. "I haven't finished yet, Mom. But I'll be along once I'm done. Promise."

Bernadette points a finger at me. "You make sure she comes soon, Mister. Or else!"

"I'll do my best, Ma'am," I tell her.

She disappears.

And it's just the two of us again.

Waiting our turn.

AUTHOR'S NOTE

THANK YOU FOR reading *Family Bonds*. I hope you enjoyed it!

This story is part of a series. I'm having a blast writing the stories and am not ready to let Robert and Clothilde go straight away, so you can expect more of these stories to pop up. They all appear first in *Pulphouse Fiction Magazine* before I publish them individually.

There's also a series of novels in the same universe, with the same characters (where they get to investigate their own murders!) so make sure to look out for those. The first book is called *Beyond the Grave*.

If you liked the story, you might want to check out some of my other books mentioned on the next page.

R.W. Wallace
www.rwwallace.com

ABOUT THE AUTHOR

R.W. WALLACE WRITES in most genres, though she tends to end up in mystery more often than not. Dead bodies keep popping up all over the place whenever she sits down in front of her keyboard.

The stories mostly take place in Norway or France; the country she was born in and the one that has been her home for two decades. Don't ask her why she writes in English—she won't have a sensible answer for you.

Her Ghost Detective short story series appears in *Pulphouse Magazine*, starting in issue #9.

You can find all her books, long and short, all genres, on rwwallace.com.

Also by R.W. Wallace

Mystery

Ghost Detective Novels
Beyond the Grave
Unveiling the Past
Beneath the Surface

Ghost Detective Shorts
Just Desserts
Lost Friends
Family Bonds
Common Ground
Till Death
Family History
Heritage
Eternal Bond
New Beginnings
Severed Ties

The Tolosa Mystery Series
The Red Brick Haze
The Red Brick Cellars
The Red Brick Basilica

Short Story Collections
Deep Dark Secrets
A Thief in the Night

Short Stories
Cold Blue Eternity
Hidden Horrors

Critters
Gertrude and the Trojan Horse
First Impressions
Let Them Eat Cake
Out of Sight
Sitting Duck
Two's Company
Like Mother Like Daughter

Time Travel Secrets (short stories)
Moneyline Secrets
Family Secrets

Romance

French Office Romance Series
Flirting in Plain Sight
Hiding in Plain Sight
Loving in Plain Sight

Short Stories
Down the Memory Aisle

Holiday Short Stories
Morbier Impossible
A Second Chance
The Magic of Sharing
The Case of the Disappearing Gingerbread City
The Lucia Crown

Young Adult (short stories)
Unexpected Consequences
The Art of Pretending
First Impressions

www.ingramcontent.com/pod-product-compliance
Lightning Source LLC
LaVergne TN
LVHW041717060526
838201LV00043B/782